Frisker

Story by Mary Lauer Nowak

Pictures by Leonard Shortall

Merrigold Press
Racine, Wisconsin

Frisker was a little black and white puppy. He lived in a kennel with many other dogs.

There were big strong dogs, and dogs you could hold on your lap. There were dogs with straight hair and dogs with curly hair. There were black dogs and white dogs and brown dogs. Oh, you never saw so many dogs!

Every day people came to see them. Almost every day, someone chose a dog for his very own. Frisker always tried to look just right, because he wanted ever so much to be chosen.

One day a farmer came.
"Oh, I would like to live
with him," Frisker thought.
He wagged his tail and
wiggled all over.
He jumped up to
lick the farmer's
hand.

"This is a friendly puppy," the farmer said. "But I need a big strong dog. I'll take that big collie."

And away went the collie to help the farmer every day with his work.

Frisker was happy for the collie. But he was sad for himself. "Next time, I must try to look strong," Frisker decided.

Soon a circus clown came. Frisker sat up very tall.

But the clown said, "I can't use that dog. I want a playful dog. I need a dog who can learn tricks." He chose a terrier and taught him a trick right there!

Now Frisker thought he knew just what to do. Every day he practiced tricks. He learned to roll over and play dead.

He learned
to sit
up and
"speak."
He was
so smart!

One morning a policeman came to the kennel. He watched Frisker do all his tricks. The policeman laughed and laughed!

"You are a very funny dog," he said. "I would like to buy you, but I need a dog who looks cross. I need a dog to guard a big store at night." So the policeman chose a police dog who certainly did look cross.

Frisker practiced looking cross all the next day. He growled. He snarled. He showed his teeth! While he was practicing, a lady came up to look at him.

"Deary me, this dog will never do," the lady said. "I want a beautiful dog. I want a dog who can win a blue ribbon in the dog show."

The lady chose a French poodle
with curly hair, and took him home.
And do you know what? The French
poodle won a blue ribbon at the dog
show, and a silver cup, too!

Poor Frisker! "No one will ever, ever choose me," he thought. It was a lonesome feeling.

One day, a little girl and boy came to the kennel. They looked at big dogs

and small dogs,

shaggy dogs

and smooth dogs.

Then they looked at Frisker!

Frisker was so happy to see them,
he wiggled all over. He wagged his
tail. He even jumped up to lick their
faces!

"Oh, I like this dog!" said the little boy. And the little girl said, "Let's take him home with us!"

So they did! And after that
Frisker was happy all day long,
because—

He was as helpful as a collie dog,
waking the family in the morning
and bringing in the newspaper at
night.

He was as clever as a circus dog,
doing all his tricks for the neighbor
children.

He was as brave as a police dog,
guarding the house while his family
slept.

Of course, he never did win a blue ribbon or a silver cup at the dog show, as the French poodle had. But the little boy and the little girl didn't care one bit about that. They liked Frisker just exactly the way he was!